A
Gift
of
Angels

Books by Jerry Bledsoe

The World's Number One, Flat-Out, All-Time Great Stock Car
Racing Book, 1975
You Can't Live on Radishes, 1976
Just Folks, 1980
Where's Mark Twain When We Really Need Him?, 1982
Carolina Curiosities, 1984
From Whalebone to Hothouse, 1986
Bitter Blood, 1988
Country Cured, 1989
North Carolina Curiosities, 1990
The Bare-Bottomed Skier, 1990
Blood Games, 1991
Blue Horizons, 1993
Before He Wakes, 1994
The Angel Doll, 1996
Death Sentence, 1998
North Carolina Curiosities, 2nd Edition, 1999
A Gift of Angels, 1999

Anthologies containing Jerry Bledsoe's work

Pete & Shirley, the Great Tar Heel Novel, 1995
Books of Passage, 1996
Close to Home, 1996
The Outer Banks, 1998
No Hiding Place, 1999

JERRY BLEDSOE

A Gift of Angels

Sequel
to

The Angel Doll
A Christmas Story

ILLUSTRATED BY TIM RICKARD

Down Home Press, Asheboro, N.C.

for Mary Beth

Acknowledgements

*I am indebted to the following dear friends
who read this book in manuscript and offered
encouragement and helpful suggestions:
Sarah Avery, Mary Beth Gibson, Beth Hennington,
Sarah Sue Ingram, Dot Jackson, Maria Johnson,
Phil Link, Patty McQuillan, Greta Medlin,
Carolyn Sakowski, Martha Jane and John Wilkinson.
Also my wife, Linda, without whom I could
accomplish nothing.*

Friendship is Love without his wings.

George Noel Gordon, Lord Byron

Prologue

A time comes when you suddenly realize that you have more friends dead than alive. Then friendship takes on new dimensions, becomes more precious, its loss more deeply mourned.

Ironically, it was the death of my oldest friend that led me back to my first lost friendship. Surely, fate meant to entwine the lives of Mutt Burton and Whitey Black, separated by so many years in my life, even though neither ever heard of the other.

What polar opposites these friendships were, one brief and intense, its youthful power unrealized at the time, the other long, comfortable and deeply satisfying. Yet both affected my life profoundly, and the loss of each, one by separation, the other by death, nearly half a century apart, scarred my heart.

Perhaps it was sorrow that caused these two disparate friendships to be joined. I know only this: Their coming together brought me a lasting gift—a little book called *The Angel Doll*—that serves as my daily reminder that the power of friendship, like that of love in all its forms, endures far beyond loss and death.

Part I

Mutt

A friend may well be reckoned the
masterpiece of Nature.

Ralph Waldo Emerson

The great man is he who does not lose
his child's heart.

Mencius

One

I could offer nobody a brighter wish than that they could have known my friend William C. "Mutt" Burton (the nickname came from a long-ago comic strip character whose ears were almost as prominent as Mutt's).

I was only twenty-six, just starting in the newspaper business, when I first met him. He was fifty-eight, my age now, but that didn't keep us from becoming fast friends. I don't think either of us was ever really aware of an age difference.

We shared too many similar loves— laughter being near the top of the list. Mutt's wit was keen, his quips forever memorable, his ear for a good joke always alert, his recall of complicated and hilarious limericks phenomenal; and the theatrics he added to his masterful story-telling made everything funnier and more entertaining.

I've encountered few people so gifted as Mutt. He was an artful photographer, a graceful writer, a brilliant actor. It seemed unlikely that a person could successfully pursue all these fields in the little tobacco town of Reidsville, North Carolina, where he was born and reared, a grocer's son, but Mutt not only managed it; he took great delight in proving it possible. He simply loved Reidsville and never wanted to leave.

He made a living writing about his town and its people for a newspaper in the nearby city of Greensboro. His Sunday column, "Professor Burton's Class," was widely beloved.

Occasionally, Mutt took a photograph for the newspaper, but photography was primarily a hobby. He took great joy in photographing circuses, as well as the company of every play in which he appeared. He was always focusing his camera on friends and promising to send them the prints he turned out in his cramped basement darkroom, but a serious case of procrastination usually kept that from happening for so long that by the time the snapshots arrived the subjects had aged beyond recognizing themselves.

No matter, the photos were always superb. I don't know that Mutt ever had an exhibit of his photographs, but he should have, for his were the equal of many of the great professionals' I have seen. His friend the poet Carl Sandburg was the brother-in-law of the famous portrait photographer Edward Steichen, but Sandburg's favorite photo of himself was made by Mutt.

If Mutt had been forced to choose between writing, picture taking or acting—and thank goodness, he never had to—there is no doubt what his choice would have been, for his love of theater came before all but the love of family and friends—and maybe chocolate, or coconut cake made with freshly grated coconut.

Nobody who saw Mutt on stage was likely to forget it—or to doubt that he could have made it on Broadway, or in Hollywood, if he had desired. But Mutt saw no point in suffering the stress and disappointments of such a career—not to mention the places in which he would have had to pursue it—when he could perform to his heart's content to greatly appreciative audiences in regional and university theaters and remain in a place that he loved.

So he became a member of the original company of the State Theater of North Carolina at Flat Rock, south of Asheville, (where he met Carl Sandburg, who lived just down the road, and where he appeared with such well-known actors as Lee Marvin, Pat Hingle and Burt Reynolds). Mutt also performed every summer at the Parkway Playhouse at Burnsville, part of the theater program at Woman's College (later the University of North Carolina at Greensboro), where he was awarded an honorary doctorate, as well as at other colleges and community theaters all over the South.

A play in which Mutt appeared was assured a large audience, and when he played W.O. Gant in Thomas Wolfe's *Look*

Homeward Angel, which I saw at least a dozen times, the house was always sold out. (It was my good fortune to see one of those productions with Wolfe's younger brother, Fred, at my side, and when Mutt lurched onto the stage in the famous drunken scene as Wolfe's fictional father, Fred, elbowed me and with a little cackle said, "He's more like my daddy than my daddy was.")

All who fell under Mutt's charms, whether from the stage, through his photographs and writings, or by personal encounter, felt as if he were a friend for life. I was one of those lucky souls for whom that was actually true. And even since his death I still feel his presence, still find myself talking to him on odd occasions and expecting to hear his familiar voice when the phone rings after midnight, for he was a night person who rarely went to bed before dawn, and that was when he usually called. I have no doubt that he still influences my life. How could I not after all that has happened?

$\mathcal{T}wo$

It was said of Mutt that a big part of his charm was that he continued to cherish into old age all the things he'd loved as a child. Among these were fireworks, the circus, and mail-order catalogs.

He set off Cherry Bombs and Roman Candles on every holiday and even created special festive occasions just to appease his pyrotechnic impulses.

He and his lifelong friend Jimmy Waynick never missed a circus that came within a few hundred miles, and when the big Ringling Bros. and Barnum & Bailey show hit the Greensboro Coliseum each February, Mutt was there prowling the dressing rooms greeting old friends, and that seemed to in-clude everybody in the troupe, from lion tamers to clowns and even the human cannon-ball—a very high-caliber person, Mutt noted.

Day in and day out, however, few things gave Mutt more pleasure than mail-order catalogs. Heavens, the catalogs!

Mutt must have been on the list of every catalog marketer in the world. I wouldn't have dreamed so many existed until I saw the great stacks of catalogs all about his house. And don't think that he got them just to peruse. He ordered from them not only with regularity but with great alacrity, and sometimes even with wild abandon. He was on a first-name basis with his postman, as well as all the delivery people from UPS, RPS, and Federal Express.

His fascination with gadgets and geehaws of every type led him to order any number of wonderful, even magical, devices that were perfectly, or at least practically, useless. I dropped by his house one day to find him on the living-room floor tearing into a big cardboard box that had just arrived.

"Mutt, what have you ordered now?" I asked.

"Oh, you've got to see this thing," he said. "It's a lawn mower like none you've ever seen."

"A lawn mower? You don't have any grass."

His front yard was bare under a huge magnolia, and his back yard was a jungle that would have required chain saws and bulldozers to tame. A mere lawn mower, not even a big professional model, which this clearly was not, didn't have a prayer against it.

"Ah, but Jerry, my boy," he said. "It flies."

"A flying lawn mower?" I said in utter bewilderment.

And indeed it was. And indeed it did. We flew it all over the house, laughing with great delight. Only later when we took it to a neighbor's yard to test it against some actual grass did we discover that the cushion of air that caused it to hover just above the surface also flattened the grass underneath so that neither lawn mower blade nor grass blade ever encountered the other.

"But it does fly," Mutt said with satisfaction and no hint of disappointment.

He was never much for mowing anyway.

Three

Of all the childhood joys that Mutt cherished into old age, the most beloved were those associated with Christmas. Nobody ever loved Christmas more than Mutt did. He treasured everything about it, especially the tingling sense of anticipation in the weeks leading up to it.

He loved Reidsville's Christmas parade marking the beginning of the seasonal shopping frenzy, and he was always prowling its edges with his camera around his neck. He loved the stores piled high with goods destined to become gifts, loved the throngs that crowded the stores and the excitement their very numbers created. It was the one time of year that he preferred going out to shop to buying from catalogs, because the cheer and goodwill of the season stirred his soul.

Santa Claus was a big part of Christmas to Mutt. He was a fervent believer in the generous, bearded old gentleman in red and would tolerate no doubters. I often thought he would have willingly become a sidewalk Santa, ringing his bell for charity, if only anybody had asked. Or even a beleaguered mall Santa taking wish lists and posing for photos with screaming and terrified children.

He loved the bright lights and decorations that festooned downtown streets and almost every house, loved the nativity plays at the churches, the holiday songs on the radio and the movies on TV, especially *The Miracle on 34th Street* and *It's a Wonderful Life* starring one of his favorite actors (and my very favorite) Jimmy Stewart.

He treasured Charles Dickens and frequently gave public readings of his classic *A Christmas Carol*, and of another favorite story of the season, Truman Capote's *A Christmas Memory*. My first acquaintance with *A Christmas Memory* came from Mutt, and reading it to Linda and our son, Erik, became a Christmas Eve ritual in my own home.

The aromas of Christmas, of evergreens and peppermint sticks, of horehound and chocolate drops, of tangy kumquats and musky chestnuts, all titillated Mutt's senses and put him in the Christmas mood, but he liked none better than the sweet fragrances of cakes and cookies and spicy pies baking in the kitchen when his wife, Martha, was still alive.

Such rituals of Christmas comforted Mutt, and, of course, he had many of them.

The annual trip across the state line into the mountains of Floyd County, Virginia, to select the perfect Christmas tree was a favorite ritual. As was the family gathering to decorate the tree with shimmering lights, bright tinsel and cherished ornaments. Some may say that most of the actual decorating was done by Martha and his daughters, Martha Jane and Anna B. (and later by his grandchildren, Jason and Mo) while Mutt sat watching in his favorite chair, pipe in hand and a twinkle in his eye, but Mull, I'm sure, took a broader, theatrical, view: that ritual of this importance demanded the perspective of distance and proper direction.

For most of us the Christmas morning ritual of opening presents, and later that day of Christmas dinner with all its excesses and varied delights, marks the end of Christmas. Not so for Mutt. Everything to that point was only prelude. For Mutt, Christmas was just beginning.

Mutt, you see, was a founder of the World Wide Twelfth Night Society, whose members are fervent believers in celebrating the full twelve days of Christmas. The twelve days don't even begin until the day after Christmas. They continue until Epiphany, January 6—Old Christmas, it is called in North Carolina, where it is still observed in some remote areas. To Mutt, this was the time to truly savor Christmas, to ponder its meaning and gather resolve to carry its warmth and goodwill into the coming year.

Mutt often used the twelve days to

write about Christmas. For years, I and others, urged him to gather some of these writings into a book, and he vowed to do it, but procrastination always overwhelmed him. After years of this, I finally took it upon myself to see that it got done. By then I had left the newspaper business and started a small press, publishing regional books. A Christmas book by Mutt was on my wish list from the beginning.

Mutt's granddaughter, Anna Morehead Nelson, called "Mo," gathered as many of the pieces as she could find. And my son, Erik, collated and edited them, sometimes seamlessly melding chunks of several essays written over a period of more than thirty years into one timeless piece. My friend Tim Rickard turned out remarkable illustrations for the book, including a drawing of Santa Claus that Mutt proclaimed the best he'd ever seen, and he had seen and collected thousands in his long life.

The book was published in 1993, and we all were proud of it.

Mutt had Christmas in his bones.

It was called *Christmas in My Bones*, from an old folk expression that Mutt loved.

"It indicates a feeling which stirs—or should stir—in the human marrow at the approach of and throughout the Christmas season," he wrote. "It is a warm, gentle excitement, a quiet, rejoicing merriment that comes from deep inside and fills the heart and tingles in the blood. It comes from seeing clear winter nights filled with crisp air and brilliant stars, from bright windows in homes and shops, from candles and tinsel and gay packages and children's faces. I've got Christmas in my bones."

Indeed, he did. His bones, his blood, and especially his heart, were completely saturated with Christmas.

Four

As it turned out, the year his book was published was the last in which Mutt would spend Christmas at home, the last in which he'd indulge and savor his many Christmas rituals. He fell seriously ill before Christmas the following year and endured weeks of hospitalization. Just days before Christmas he was moved to a nursing home in an adjoining county, twenty-five miles from Reidsville.

It was grim trip that Linda, Erik and I made to see him that Christmas Eve. I hated nursing homes and wasn't sure that I could stand to see so lively a person as Mutt in such circumstances.

We arrived early in the evening, before any of his family. He was in a private room that showed no sign of Christmas, his bed cranked up so he could watch TV. He was asleep, his head sagging to one side, mouth open, and we were reluctant to wake him. But he must have sensed our presence, for he stirred and opened his eyes. He looked a bit confused at first, as if he thought perhaps we were nurses with more medicine. But then he recognized us, saw the ribbon-bedecked packages Erik and I were holding, and the triple-rich chocolate cake Linda had made for him—a different and far happier kind of medicine—and his face broke into smile.

"Merry Christmas to the Bledsoes," he called, Santa-like. "Merr-r-ry Christmas!"

We hadn't been there long before the dearth of Christmas decorations was instantly cured. We heard a commotion in the hallway, and a nurse burst through the door, her face a picture of delight.

"Mutt," she cried—not Mr. Burton; he clearly had already worked his considerable charms on the staff. "Look what somebody sent you!"

Behind her were two attendants pushing a food cart. On it was a small but gorgeously decorated Christmas tree that had just been delivered from a florist shop.

"Who on earth?" Mutt said.

"Want me to check the card?" I asked.

"By all means."

I tore it open and read, "Merry Christmas. Bob and Kay."

Bob Timberlake, an internationally known North Carolina painter and designer, had been Mutt's long-time friend and shared his love of Christmas. Bob had designed a Christmas stamp for the U.S. Postal Service, and Mutt loved his work, especially his annual Christmas paintings.

"Bless their dear hearts," Mutt said. "What a treasure are good friends."

"Isn't it beautiful?" asked the smiling nurse, gazing at the tree.

"It's that and more," Mutt agreed.

I worried that Mutt would never get out of the nursing home and knew that if that turned out to be so, his days would be short. Thankfully, it proved not to be the case. He rallied after Christmas, was moved to a rehabilitation center in Winston-Salem to begin physical therapy, and eventually was able to return home.

I hoped he'd get to spend at least one more Christmas there, but by his birthday on November 11, his eighty-eighth, he was back in the hospital. I went to the party that his daughters held for him. People had been in and out all day with gifts and flowers and well-wishes. Still the room was filled with family and friends, joking and laughing. Mutt tried to join in, but he was weak and tired and could barely speak. He was gaunt and pale, and the usual twinkle was missing from his eyes.

At one point he indicated that he wanted to speak to me privately, and the others left. I sat in a hard chair close by the head of his bed. I had no idea what he wanted to say, and I wasn't sure that I was emotionally prepared for it, whatever it might be.

I had to lean close to hear him. He hadn't been shaved and his face was covered with white stubble. I knew this was an important moment and I wanted to remember details.

"Had three nurses in here the other night," he said haltingly, his voice a hoarse whisper.

I couldn't imagine where this was headed. Mutt had an eye for the ladies.

"I said, 'Do y'all know how to play poker?'" he went on. "They said, 'No.' I said, 'Good. Can you get some cards?'"

We used to have a big, nickel-limit poker game after Mutt's shows and a couple of times a year at his house, but he always dropped out if the bet went over two cents, or a wild game was called. The game was never the point anyway. It was just an excuse for the wonderful camaraderie, the joking, story-telling and laughing.

"First hand, I turned over trip queens," Mutt said, his voice growing stronger. The twinkle was now back in his eye. "Went on to win twenty-six cents."

I laughed, took his hand and kissed him on the forehead.

"I love you," I said.

"I love you, too, old boy."

That was the only time we'd ever spoken those words to one another, and I should have known from the beginning that was what he wanted to tell me.

Early in December, the phone rang. I was writing at my cabin in the mountains of Virginia, only a few miles from the place where Mutt always came to get his Christmas trees. At first I didn't recognize the voice of my friend Phil Link, who'd been Mutt's friend from childhood. He was crying.

"I'm sorry to bother you; I know you're working," he said. "But if you want to see our old buddy Mutt alive again, you'd better come."

"Phil, Mutt Burton will not die before

Christmas," I said emphatically, but my voice was catching as I fought to control my own emotions. "The stars will fall from the heavens before that happens. He just won't die before Christmas. He may die at one minute past midnight on January seventh, but he'll live through Christmas and all the twelve days that follow."

I believed that, too.

"I hope you're right," Phil said, "but you'd better come on."

On my way down the mountains I saw a falling star.

Mutt died before I got there.

For those of us who loved him, and our numbers were many, a great part of the joy was taken from that Christmas, even though we knew Mutt wouldn't have wanted it to be that way. For me, I was certain, some of the joy of Christmas was lost forever.

$\mathcal{P}$art 2

$\mathcal{T}$he $\mathcal{A}$ngel $\mathcal{D}$oll

...Grant that I may not so much
Seek to be consoled as to console;
To be understood as to understand;
To be loved as to love;
For it is in giving that we receive....

St. Francis of Assisi

Five

I wanted to do something to pay tribute to Mutt, but I wasn't sure what. My heart told me it should have something to do with Christmas.

I, too, had always shared Mutt's love for this holiday that had seemed so much happier until his death. And in nearly a quarter of a century as a newspaper columnist, I, like Mutt, had written many pieces about it. Perhaps I could use those as the basis for a book about Christmas and dedicate it to Mutt's memory.

I started working on it the day after Christmas, just three weeks after Mutt's funeral. I began searching out old columns and decided on a title: *In Search of Christmas*.

It was then that I remembered a story

I had written my second Christmas in the newspaper business. It appeared in the small-town daily where I had been employed for just fifteen months, and which I was about to leave for a larger paper in Greensboro, where I was soon to meet Mutt. Perhaps I could work it into the book.

This was a story about a doll that became a symbol of a particular Christmas in my childhood. It happened during the great polio epidemic that brought so much fear, pain and sorrow in the late '40s and early '50s.

Whitey Black was my best friend then, and we shared a paper route in Thomasville, a furniture-manufacturing town just forty-five miles from Reidsville, where Mutt was then a middle-aged man with a family. Whitey had a little sister, Sandy, five years old, who had survived polio, but it had left her weak and susceptible to other diseases.

Sandy loved a book called *The Littlest Angel*, and Whitey read it to her frequently. When she decided that she wanted an angel doll for Christmas, he became determined to get one for her. There was just one problem: We couldn't find an angel doll anywhere.

That situation was solved when Whitey got the mother of our friend Billy Barnes to transform a regular doll into an angel. But Sandy fell ill again and died before Christmas without ever seeing or holding the doll. After Whitey and his mother left to bury her in South Carolina, from where they had moved to our town only a couple of years earlier, they never returned, and nobody in Thomasville ever heard from them again.

It was a sad story to write for Christmas, and I wasn't sure now what had prompted me to do it. I was even less sure after I searched it out in the microfilm files at the library in the town where I had worked so many years before. Not only did the story have an unhappy and unsatisfactory ending, it was poorly written. I clearly wasn't the writer then that I had fancied myself to be.

Nonetheless, I made a copy and brought the story home. Maybe I could fix it and still use it in the book. After all, several significant events had happened since then that gave the story a new and brighter ending.

Years earlier, Billy's mom had made a gift to me of the doll that she had transformed and Whitey had never claimed, and it had become an important part of Christmas for Linda, Erik and me, holding a place of honor every year beside our tree. And some years back, when I discovered that an anonymous donor sent angel dolls to a children's hospital in a distant city every Christmas, I convinced myself that Whitey was the benefactor, and that he was doing well and still showing his love for his little sister.

Anyway, when I started fiddling with the piece, hoping to improve it, an enthralling experience overcame me. I was taken back to that Christmas when I was ten, and memories welled as never before. I was reliving that time all over again, and the details fairly flew from my fingers onto the computer keyboard.

Many times I'd heard writers say that a story, or an article, or a book had seemed to write itself—that they had little to do with it. I had never believed that, because nothing like that had ever happened to me. Writing was always a struggle that I faced with great reluctance and quit with immense relief. But now such was my excitement that I had to force myself to leave the computer in the early morning hours each night to get a few hours sleep.

And when I finally tapped out the final sentence, I burst into tears and sat sobbing uncontrollably. I didn't know why, but I couldn't stop. Surely I was crying for Sandy, and for Whitey and his family, and most certainly for Mutt, for whom I had not yet allowed myself to grieve fully. Maybe I was crying for all the sad stories I'd ever heard.

Now I think that some of my tears must also have been from unrecognized joy, joy for the hope that this little story gave, and joy for the promise that Christmas brought to all who would accept it.

I knew one thing for certain: This story, if you'll pardon the expression, had taken wing on its own. It could not be part of any collection. It had to stand alone. *The Angel Doll*, as I now titled it, would be Mutt's book.

Six

Reliving Whitey's story so soon after Mutt's death set me thinking about friendship as I never had before.

I ticked off other close friends I'd lost to death in recent years: Jim McAllister, Roy Rabon, Tom Miller, Bob Zschiesche, Ed "Creole" Davis, Tom McDonald, Leon Bullock, Kays Gary, George Anderson, Hubert Breeze (and soon was to come another, James "Tiny" Weeks), most of them dead at an age younger than I am now. It seemed that almost every encounter with somebody from my childhood, or from my high school class, brought news of the passing of another old friend or acquaintance.

As hard as it was to deal with losing friends to death, I at least had the consolation that I had no control over that, no responsibility for my loss. But I was all too aware that my own failures had cost me far more friends.

I was no longer close to a single friend from childhood, high school, the Army, early jobs. And many more recent friends had slipped from my life as well. Some had been so close at the time that I couldn't have imagined living out my life without them.

In most cases, no particular moment had defined the end of these friendships. No angry arguments, no harsh words, no hurt feelings. Usually there had been no intention for the relationship to die. So many factors intervened. Other interests developed. Children arrived. Jobs changed and required more work. People succeeded, or failed, or moved away. Life got too hectic. Time flew.

At first, there had been occasional visits, calls now and then, promises to get together soon, cards at Christmas. But gradually they diminished, and eventually disappeared, the friendships surviving only in memory.

Mutt's death focused my regret about this, reminded me how much I missed so many of these once dear friends. Some had been gone now for many years and I had no idea even where they were. Surely with just a little effort some of these relationships could have been saved, could have continued to bless my life.

My friend Jim McAllister had been very wise about such matters. He knew that friend-ship had to be nurtured to thrive. He was al-ways planning special and recurring events for old and distant friends, events that became tradition and kept all of us in touch.

I thought I had learned that lesson from him. For years after his death, I and others continued some of the events he originated, but one by one people dropped out, and the events eventually fell with them, as did many of the friendships.

Now I was at the point where I was making no new friends—and couldn't stand the thought of losing the few who remained. I could do nothing about those robbed from me by death, but I certainly could do more to see that no other friendships withered and died from inattention.

The question that arose was whether I could revive any of those already atrophied. Had too much time elapsed, too many things changed? It would be awkward, perhaps, but I could only try. And I already knew where I had to begin: with Whitey, my first lost friendship. The book I had just finished made that imperative.

But how would I find him? And why hadn't I already tried?

I had made only a cursory effort years earlier when I had first learned of the angel dolls at the children's hospital and surmised that Whitey had to be the anonymous donor. After a few calls I had given up. Had I really wanted to find him? Or was I fearful that I actually might?

A few times, by sheer happenstance, I had encountered old friends after long separations only to discover that beyond catching up on the past, we had nothing in common, no bind to continue to hold us together, indeed many reasons to remain apart. In those cases the sorrow of discovery had been greater than the sorrow of separation.

Would such be the case with Whitey? Would in finding him I learn things that I really did not want to know? Would our relationship be better in memory than in reality?

I pushed such questions aside. This time I was determined to find him no matter the consequences.

Although I had been a reporter for thirty years, I really had no idea how to seek out a lost person. During my newspaper days, I had written several happy stories about people who had finally found others for whom they'd been searching. Usually, these were siblings separated early in their lives, and often it had taken decades for them to find one another again. The reunions had always been joyous, but I never had gone back later to see if they remained so.

I had no illusions that my search would be easy. At the time, I had not yet been introduced to the wonders of the Internet with its vast possibilities for seeking out lost souls, and as it turned out, that was just as well, for it would have been no help to me. I began in the only way I knew: by searching in the place I had last known him to be, South Carolina.

I worked by telephone, calling information in all the major cities and asking for numbers of Blacks, James, Jimmy, Jim, J. Sometimes there would be dozens of them, and I could get only two at a time. I usually called in the evening on weekdays when I figured most people would be at home. I interrupted a lot of dinners and favorite TV shows and got a few grumps, but many more people were friendly and willing to listen and offer suggestions. None, however, was Whitey, or knew anything about him. After going through the major cities without success—and running up huge phone bills—I realized the futility of my effort. How many small towns were there in South Carolina where he might be? And how many other places on the face of the earth? And what if his phone number weren't listed?

I bought a book on finding missing persons and finally consulted a detective friend. Neither was reassuring. Indeed, both made me more aware of the extent of my problem.

I didn't even know Whitey's real name. Was it Jimmy, or Jim, or James? Was one of the three actually his middle name? Might he now be going by a name I'd never known? Furthermore, if I had ever known his birth date, I couldn't remember it. I knew that it probably had fallen sometime between November 1 and December 31, 1941.

Without the certainty of name and birth date, I learned, my chances of finding Whitey after so many years were slim to none. It likely would come down to calling Blacks around the country for the rest of my days and still not finding him.

It came to me then that perhaps *The Angel Doll* would be the answer. Maybe Whitey would read it, or hear about it, or somebody who knew him would, and he would seek me out. I could only hope that might be the case.

But as time went on I wasn't sure that would be a possibility either. I began to doubt that *The Angel Doll* ever would find an audience big enough to matter.

Seven

I had been very hopeful when my agent sent *The Angel Doll* to publishers. I'd never felt so confident about a book, certain that this story had a power that would touch many people. The first rejection came after a couple of weeks. Soon others were arriving with numbing regularity. Rejection by rejection, my confidence descended into depression, bottoming with the call from my agent telling me that all the major publishers and even the smaller houses to which he had sent it had passed.

How, I wondered, could I have been so wrong in thinking this story special?

Yet, as low as I felt, I was not about to give up. I'd seen the reaction the story brought from friends who read it. Major publishers had been wrong before, I told myself; oftentimes, they had no idea what appealed to people far removed from New York.

Perhaps this was a story that could be appreciated only by people who had grown up in small towns in the South in the '50s, but there were a lot of them, and they should have the chance to accept or reject it for themselves. I suspected, though, that the lost innocence and disappearing values of that era and that way of life might reach far beyond that generation and that region.

I decided to add the book to the fall list of my own little regional press and see what happened. It would have limited distribution, offering no hope for big sales. And it would be far less helpful in locating Whitey than if a national publisher brought it out. But if he had remained in the Carolinas or Virginia, it still might reach him.

The book's reception that fall was far greater than I ever dreamed, bringing me more wonderful and moving experiences than any book I'd ever written. But it did not find

Whitey.

I spent nearly four months on the road promoting the book. Wherever I went, people who had read it asked the same questions over and over. "Have you heard from Whitey?" "Have you found Whitey?"

"Not yet," I'd tell them, for I still had hope.

Some even demanded, "Why haven't you found him?"

"I'm trying," I replied, and indeed I was. Whenever I did interviews with newspaper reporters, or at TV and radio stations, I always mentioned that I was looking for Whitey, and that I hoped that anybody who had information about him would call or write. Yet I heard nothing. It was my only disappointment about the book.

The Angel Doll was such a big success regionally that it attracted a major publisher the following year. I spent most of that year frantically trying to meet my deadline on a crime book on which I'd been working for nearly three years. I finished just in time to strike out on the road again promoting the new edition of *The Angel Doll*.

This time the book was available nationwide. Three book clubs had selected it, and in November it would be excerpted in *Good Housekeeping* magazine. If I had any genuine chance of turning up Whitey, this surely was it.

The reaction to the book was as warm and wonderful as it had been the year before, except that this time it came from all over the country instead of just one little part of the South. Letters and calls came every week—but none offered any hint to Whitey's whereabouts.

The most touching and meaningful messages came from a doll maker in Santa Fe, a crafts group in Birmingham, and a woman in San Diego, all of whom sent word that the book had moved them to begin making angel dolls and taking them to the children's wards of their local hospitals at Christmas. What a tribute to Whitey and

Sandy, I thought. Wouldn't it be wonderful if people in every town and city started doing the same thing?

I wanted Whitey to know about this, but the truth was that by this time I had given up hope of ever finding him. Still, I continued the effort wherever I went.

Less than three weeks before Christmas I arrived at The Open Book in Greenville, South Carolina, for an autographing. An old friend, Tom Gower, owned the store. He had been one of a handful of booksellers who had invited me for a signing when my first book, which was about stock car racing, came out nearly a quarter of a century earlier (we sold a grand total of two copies, I remember). I always enjoyed going to Tom's store and visiting with him, and now we were even selling a few more books.

My signing was to be from four to six in the afternoon, but I arrived fifteen minutes early for a scheduled TV interview. The young reporter was waiting with her cameraman, lights in place. She had received a copy of

The Angel Doll for Christmas the year before, she told me, and had loved it. She wanted to include this interview in a Christmas feature she was planning. Her last question was this: "I'm dying to know, have you heard from Whitey?"

I went into my stock routine, trying not to betray my hopelessness.

Some customers had arrived while the interview was under way, and as soon as it was finished, I began signing books while the reporter and her cameraman packed to leave. I was chatting with a woman who wanted four copies as Christmas gifts for nieces and nephews when the reporter bade me farewell. I had signed the four copies and was thanking the woman for coming when I saw two big and striking blue eyes framed by curly blonde hair peering up at me from just above the table top.

"Why, hello there," I said to the little girl, who was dressed in pink and white and looked to be five or so. "What's your name?"

She was clearly shy and turned her

A Gift of Angels – 61

head into her mother's dress.

Her mother, too, was blonde and attractive, perhaps thirty.

"Can't you tell him your name?" she said, smiling down at her daughter.

"Mmm-uh," said the girl with a nod.

"Well, go ahead."

"Laurel," she said so quickly that I almost missed it.

"Oh, what a pretty name," I said. "Did you know that laurel is a flower?"

"Mmm-uh," she said with a nod.

"It grows in the mountains. It's one of my favorite flowers. And you're just as pretty as it is."

A bashful smile came over her face.

"Can't you say thank you?" her mother asked.

"Mmm-uh."

"You remind me of a little girl I knew
a long, long time ago."

"Well, go ahead."

"You're welcome," she said with a grin, bringing laughs from her mother and me and several of the people in line.

"You know, you remind me of a little girl I knew a long, long time ago," I told her.

"I bet I know just who you're thinking about," her mother said, taking me by surprise. "I was named for her. I'm Sandra Medlin. Everybody calls me Sandy. Whitey was my father."

Eight

I must have looked stunned, for that was precisely my feeling as I stared in disbelief at this beautiful young woman. Questions bubbled in my mind, all of them wanting to boil out at once. Instead, they clogged my throat, leaving me speechless.

"I didn't even know about this book until a week ago," I heard her saying. "A friend told me I ought to read it and loaned me her copy. I sat down with it just a few days ago and I couldn't believe what I was reading. I cried all the way through it. It told me so much I didn't know, made me understand so many things.

"I called my friend, and I said, 'This book is about my daddy!' She said, 'No, you're kidding.' I said, 'No, it's about my daddy,' and we both started crying I never knew that he'd been called Whitey; I'm sure my mother didn't know it either.

"I was going to try to call you, or write, and then I saw in the paper that you were going to be here, and I knew I had to come. It was the strangest feeling, almost as if I'd known all along that this was destined to be.

"My friend told me yesterday, 'An angel must have directed me to give you that book when I did.' And I said, 'I think you're right.'"

I couldn't believe this was happening either, and I still had trouble finding words.

"Can you stay until everybody's gone so we can talk?" I finally managed to ask.

"I've got a better idea," she said. "Can you come to our house for dinner? I've got some things I'm sure you'd want to see."

"I'd love to."

"It won't be anything fancy," she warned.

"I'm sure it'll be better than Burger King, or Taco Bell, where I usually end up when I'm on the road."

"Well, maybe a little," she said with a smile.

She looked down at her daughter. "You know what's really eerie?"

"What?"

"Guess what her favorite book is."

"*The Littlest Angel*," I said without hesitation, for somehow I already knew.

She nodded. "And I didn't even know that about Sandy until I read your book. I never heard anything about the doll, and if my mother had known about that, she would have told me. Those were things he kept to himself."

"I've got to know just one thing now," I said.

"I know...."

She glanced away, hesitating for a

moment, and when her eyes turned back to mine I saw tears. "My dad was killed in Vietnam before I was born."

I must have blanched, for she suddenly reached across the table and hugged me.

"I'm sorry," she said, and I found myself speechless again.

Part 3

Whitey

He shall give his angels charge over thee, to keep thee in all thy ways.

Psalms

When the voices of children are heard on the green
And laughing is heard on the hill,
My heart is at rest within my breast
And everything else is still.

William Blake

Charity vaunteth not itself.

1 Corinthians

Nine

I was still reeling from Sandy's revelation as I drove to her house in a new and treeless subdivision outside Simpsonville, a burgeoning suburb southeast of Greenville, following a map she had hastily drawn on note paper.

The house was a two-story Tudor, built mostly of brick, flanked by azaleas and other shrubbery far from maturity. A late-model minivan and a compact Buick were parked in the driveway. All the outside lights were on, and I saw an elaborate wooden gym-set with a yellow plastic sliding board and a tiny, cedar-shingled playhouse in the fenced back yard. I couldn't help thinking of the sharp contrast between Whitey's childhood and his granddaughter's.

Sandy's husband answered the bell. He was a few years older than she, a handsome, friendly man with a receding hairline, who obviously spent time in a gym himself. He was an executive at a synthetic textile plant that sprawled alongside I-85, I was soon to learn, and he appeared to have arrived home from work just in time to shed his suit coat, roll his shirt sleeves, unbutton his collar and loosen his tie to greet an unexpected guest.

"Gene Medlin," he said, offering his hand. "Welcome. Come in."

Sandy quickly appeared in a doorway leading to the kitchen, wiping her hands on her apron, Laurel tagging close behind.

"I hope you like lasagna," she called.

"Love it."

"It'll be ready in just a little bit," she said, as her husband led me into the living room, a room clearly not often used from the looks of the showroom-fresh furniture and the pristine carpet. I noticed photo albums and scrapbooks piled on the coffee table alongside a shoe box. A Bob Timberlake winter scene above the sofa offered a starting point for small talk until Sandy appeared to announce that dinner was served.

Over the next hour and a half, as we ate and talked in the dining room, I began to fill in some of the unanswered questions from the past.

After leaving Thomasville, Whitey's mother had returned to Easley, South Carolina, a cotton-mill town in the hilly country about twelve miles west of Greenville where she and Whitey moved in with her parents until she got a job at the mill and, eventually, a place of her own. When Whitey was twelve, she remarried. Her husband was an older man who died of emphysema only three years later, leaving his wife and stepson a mill house and a modest pension. "My mother said that my dad once told her that his main memory of those three years was of unending coughing," Sandy said.

It was no surprise to me that Whitey

had worked through all his years at Easley High, first delivering the *Greenville News*, then stocking shelves and bagging groceries at Pickensville Grocery, which the locals still called Welborn's, after Claude Welborn, who had been its first owner. Whitey also had hopped curb on weekend nights at The Drive-In on Liberty Drive. Following his graduation in 1960, he had been accepted at Clemson University, and while he was there two of the most significant events of his life took place. To help with tuition, he signed up for ROTC. And at a football game in Columbia with arch-rival USC during his junior year, he met Laurel Wingate, a nursing student.

"So Laurel is named for your mother," I said.

Sandy nodded. "We were very close. I guess that's what happens when you've never known your father."

"Where's your mom now?" I asked.

"She died a year ago of cancer."

"I'm sorry," I said, embarrassed for

bringing it up.

"She was sick for eighteen months," Sandy said. "I was working when she first got sick, but I quit so I could be with her. She had nursed so many people so lovingly through her life, and I was determined that she was going to get the same kind of care from me.

"She lived alone. She never remarried. I think she thought that she could never find anybody she could love as much as she loved my dad. After she got sick, we moved her in here, and except for the time she was in the hospital in Greenville, where she had worked for so many years, she was right here with us. I think she lived longer than she would have, just from being with Laurel."

She paused for a moment to compose herself.

"I didn't go back to work after Mother died because I thought it was more important for me to be with Laurel. We'd been planning to have another child, but we put it off after Mother got sick."

She smiled at her husband across the table. "We've been talking about it again. We always wanted a girl and a boy."

"What am I going to do with all that baseball stuff I've already bought if we have another girl?" her husband said teasingly.

"Well, I guess you'll just have to teach your daughters to play baseball, won't you?"

We laughed, and Sandy went back to talking about her father. From the time he met her mother, she said, he drove his yellow and white '57 Plymouth to Columbia at every opportunity, but not nearly as often as he would have liked. In addition to his studies and ROTC responsibilities, he also worked during his college years, consuming almost all his free time, and he even managed to send money to his mother to help with medical bills and other expenses.

Whitey got a degree in history in May of 1965 and was soon commissioned a second lieutenant in the U.S. Army. He was assigned as a platoon commander in a basic training battalion at Fort Jackson, just outside

Columbia, the same battalion, although not the same company, in which I had spent nine miserable weeks as an E-1 recruit more than five years earlier.

That fall, Whitey married Laurel Wingate on her birthday at her church, First Baptist, where her father was the minister, in her hometown of Chester, fifty-five miles north of Columbia.

"Why don't we go to the living room?" Sandy suggested. "I've got their wedding photographs. Would you like coffee?"

"I'll pass on the coffee, thanks. That dinner almost did me in. I ate too much. It was terrific."

Laurel had been excused from the table well before dessert and had gone to sleep in front of the TV in the den, holding a stuffed replica of the Cookie Monster. Her father carried her to her room, while Sandy and I settled on the sofa with the photo albums and scrapbooks. Gene returned shortly. "I'm sorry," he said, "but I have some work that I absolutely have to get done before tomorrow morning. Would it be okay if I leave you two to talk?"

"Of course," I said rising. "Will I see you before I go?"

"Oh, sure," he said. "We'd love to have you spend the night. We have two bedrooms going unused."

"Thank you," I said, "but I checked into a hotel before I went to the bookstore. All my stuff is over there."

"Well, you're welcome any time. I'll see you a little later."

I sat back down and Sandy reached for one of the photo albums.

"Mother put these together because she wanted me to know everything possible about my dad," she said. "When I was little we had regular sessions where she would talk about him, and we would go through these albums and I would identify the people in the photos and repeat everything she'd ever told me about them."

The wedding photos were like all other wedding photos, mostly stiff and posed. The bride was in a standard white gown with a lace bodice, a long train, and the traditional veil. Whitey was in full-dress uniform, ramrod straight and looking uncomfortable, but I would have recognized him anywhere.

Freckles still sprinkled his nose; and his hair, what there was of it, was still blonde and trimmed little differently from the crude crewcuts that my dad used to give to me, my brother and Whitey with the electric clippers he bought to save the fifty-cent fee charged by Thomasville barbers for kids' haircuts.

In some of the photos, Whitey didn't seem so tense and posed, especially in the one in which he was gazing into his bride's sparkling eyes before their first kiss as husband and wife. In other shots, both were laughing, arms interlocked, exchanging sips of sherbet punch and wedding cake.

"They look as if they adored one another," I said.

"They did," Sandy confirmed.

We continued through page after page of wedding photos, Sandy identifying all the people. I recognized Whitey's mother as soon as I saw her, but she looked even more gaunt than when I'd known her, and much older. Her fancy dress seemed to hang on her lank frame.

"Is she still living?" I asked.

"No, I never knew her either. She had a stroke and died before my dad went to Vietnam, while he was stationed at Fort Benning."

She picked up another album. "Until your book, this was all I had of my dad's early life," she said. "I think his mother put this together. After she died, he had to come back to Easley and take care of things. He sold the house and most of the furniture. And he packed up her personal belongings and took them to his grandmother's house. She later gave some of those things to my mother."

She handed the album to me. I didn't recognize any of the people or scenes in the aging snapshots in the first part of the book— and Sandy had no idea who they were either—but then I came upon a fading snap-shot, creased and cracked where it apparently had been accidentally folded. There stood Whitey and Sandy posing on a front porch. The brace was clear on Sandy's leg.

"That was the house where they lived in Thomasville," I told Sandy. "I was over there all the time. That had to have been made not long before Sandy died."

"I never knew where that had been taken," she said. "But isn't it amazing how much Sandy looks like Laurel there?"

"It is," I agreed.

I came upon several more shots of Whitey, most of them in his teen years. In one he was in a baseball uniform, "Easley" spelled out across the shirt, crouched in fielding position.

"He played in a mill league," Sandy said.

In another he wore a soiled white apron over his jeans and a paper cap with R.C. Cola advertised on it, posing in front of The Drive-in with another boy, similarly attired, their arms around each other's shoulders, both with silly grins.

Whitey affected a James Dean pose in another shot, wearing a T-shirt with the sleeves rolled to his shoulders, a semi-sneer on his lips, his left foot propped on the front bumper of either a '49 or a '50 Ford coupe.

"Mom said that was his first car," Sandy said. "He paid for it himself."

One shot had "Junior-Senior, 1959, Easley High" scribbled across the bottom. In it Whitey looked ill at ease in a white sport coat with sleeves that drooped nearly to his thumbs and a lapel that sported a wilting carnation. He was wearing dark pants and white shoes and standing beside a plump girl in a gaudy evening gown with puffed sleeves and a sour look on her face. They appeared to be in a school gym beneath an arbor covered with artificial flowers.

"Well, at least he went to the prom," I said. "I never got up nerve enough to ask anybody."

"From the looks of him, I'd say he wished he hadn't either," Sandy said with a laugh.

Tucked into the back of the album was Whitey's baby book. In it his mother had recorded the date and time of his birth, his weight (six pounds, eight ounces), his length (nineteen inches) his favorite foods (oatmeal and apple sauce), his first words (Da-Da). He'd crawled at eleven months, taken his first step at fourteen. A lock of his fair and delicate hair, preserved in cigarette-pack cellophane, was tucked between the pages where the date of his first haircut was recorded.

As I put down the album, Sandy handed me another, this one filled with photos made after her mother and father were married.

"That was their first little duplex apartment in Columbia," she said of a shot of her mother sitting on the stoop, smiling, her right hand over her face, peeking between two fingers at the camera.

There were black-and-white shots of each of them on the white sand beach at Panama City, Florida, and one of them together, laughing and romping in the emerald surf in what now appeared to be antique swimsuits. There were shots of their first Christmas together, proudly holding up their presents from one another.

A professional eight-by-ten photo showed Whitey marching with his troops at a military ceremony. In another, Laurel was earnestly attempting to pin a first lieutenant's silver bar onto the shoulder of his uniform, while a captain, his company commander, looked on smiling. A far less professional snapshot caught Whitey engulfed in smoke as he rescued hamburgers from a flaming charcoal grill at a party celebrating his promotion.

"I don't think any two people were ever happier together than my mother and dad," Sandy said.

Near the back of the album was a green-tinted color Polaroid of Whitey in uniform walking briskly toward an airport ticket agent, a briefcase in one hand, his ticket in the other. In a second shot he had turned at the entrance of the ramp to give a little wave, a forlorn look on his face.

"That was in Atlanta when he left for Vietnam," Sandy told me. "I think one of my uncles took those. My mother held up for his sake until he got on the plane, but my grandmother said they practically had to carry her back to the car. She stayed in bed crying for three days and hardly ate a bite. But when he called her from San Francisco, she was up in a flash, pretending that she was perfectly okay and telling him how much she loved him."

"When was that?" I asked.

"It was near the end of October, nineteen sixty-seven."

"And when was he killed?"

"Not quite four months later. On February thirteenth. It was a Tuesday. My mother was still working at the hospital in Columbus, Georgia. Two officers came to tell her."

Gene rejoined us then. "Did you get it all done, Honey?" Sandy asked.

"Most of it," he said with an air of frustration. "It's a report I have due tomorrow," he said to me in explanation.

I glanced at my watch and was surprised that it was nearly midnight.

"My goodness," I said. "I didn't know it was so late. I've taken up your whole evening. I just didn't realize time was flying so fast."

"Oh, no problem, no problem," Gene said.

"We're just happy to have you here," Sandy said. "It's been good for me. There's so much we haven't talked about yet, though."

"I would like to know how your dad died," I said. "Do you know any details?"

"It's all in here," she said, reaching for the shoe box. She removed the top to reveal bundles of letters still in their envelopes, wrapped with rubber bands.

"What's your schedule tomorrow?" she asked.

"Well, I have to be in Columbia for a radio interview at four o'clock, then I have a signing at the Happy Bookseller tomorrow night."

"Could you come back here in the morning?"

"I could."

"Would you like to take these letters and look through them tonight? You could bring them back in the morning and we could drive over to Easley to the cemetery if you'd like."

"I'd like that very much," I said.

Ten

I felt no need for sleep, even though it was well past midnight. Propped against the headboard of the king-size bed in my hotel room, shoes off, all lights blazing, CNN on the TV, I sat sifting through the letters in the shoe box. Clearly, Sandy's mother had kept every letter that Whitey had written to her from Vietnam.

They were bundled by the month, November, December, January, each bundle holding at least a dozen letters. The February stack, however, was noticeably thin: just two.

Only a few letters into the first batch I saw a pattern. Whitey was never going to tell his wife anything that would cause her worry. He wrote about his arrival at Ton Son Nhut

Air Base, about the heat, about the incredible beauty of the country, about what a fascinating and cosmopolitan city Saigon was.

"The smell is the only thing I can't get used to," he wrote in one early letter. "I wish I could describe it. It hangs over everything, heavy and oppressive, like some rancid sweet and sour sauce. But after a while you get used to it enough that you don't notice it quite so much."

Usually the letters were very personal. He wrote about how much he missed her, how much he loved her, how much he looked forward to her letters, how he wondered if he could make it a whole year without her. "But every day that passes is a day I'm closer to being with you again," he added in his customary way of never neglecting the positive.

Often he recalled special moments from their past, and sometimes these passages were so intensely private that I felt myself intruding and skipped them.

The closest Whitey ever came to mentioning any kind of conflict or possible danger in his early letters was a single sentence he wrote not long after his arrival: "It's such a pretty place, and sometimes it seems so tranquil that it's hard to imagine there's a war going on."

He always closed on an optimistic note: "Don't worry about me, Baby Doll. I'm just fine. Stay as sweet and wonderful and beautiful as you've always been until I can have you in my arms again. Meanwhile, keep those cards and letters coming!"

On a Sunday night in late November, he wrote: "I don't think I've told you anything about the children. That's what impresses me most about this place. They can be dirty and hungry and half naked in ragged clothes, but they're always smiling. A lot of them don't have fathers, and some of them, heaven only knows what their mothers do. Some of them just seem to live on the street. They come swarming around us wherever we go. Yeah, they usually want something. Candy, or gum, or coins, or rations. Gimme, gimme. But they're so open and so friendly that it's hard not to respond to them."

Ten days later, he wrote, "I've started carrying gum and candy for the kids. I'm a real hit! You'd think I was Howdy Doody!"

Laurel must have joked with him about that, because in a later letter he remarked, "OK, so maybe I do look a little like Howdy Doody, but you're the only one who'll ever pull my strings."

"WHAT A WAY TO FIND OUT I'M GOING TO BE A FATHER!!!!!" he began a letter dated December 14. "P.S. I'M PREGNANT!

"Oh, Baby Doll, you can't imagine what those words did to me. My chest was pounding so hard that before I could say, 'Be still, my heart,' it flopped right out of my mouth and I had to go chasing after it hollering, 'Please, my heart, slow down just a little bit so I can catch up!...'

"I knew something wonderful was going to come from that last night we had together. As sad as I was about having to leave you, those were the most precious hours of my life, and now they are even more precious.

But we are going to have many more precious hours—and days!—and months!—and years!—together, and now we'll have a little boy, or a little girl—or, who knows?, maybe two or three of each—to share them with us. I wish I was there to give you a big hug and show you exactly how I feel. I can't believe it! I'M GOING TO BE A DADDY!!!! I love you both."

In every subsequent letter, Whitey expressed his joy and excitement about Laurel's pregnancy, always admonishing her to take care of herself. "I know how much you love your work," he wrote, "but you can't keep going now as hard as you did before. I know it helps you to keep your mind off things, but you just have to slow down and take it a little easier. You can't spend so many hours on your feet. And remember: EAT YOUR VEGETABLES!"

One letter was dated "Christmas Day, 1967."

"Sure doesn't seem like Christmas, probably because I'm not with you. And I haven't exactly adjusted yet to 80-degree Christmases. And the decorations here leave a little to be desired. We do have Christmas trees, but they're not exactly like the ones back home, and some of them are a little peculiarly decorated to say the least. Only in Vietnam.

"I did go to a Christmas Eve service last night, and we sang 'Silent Night' and several other carols. It reminded me of being at your dad's church on Christmas Eve. But my best Christmas experience came a couple of days ago. Some of the guys and I pitched in and bought a bunch of cheap toys and hair brushes and things like that, and we wrapped them up and took them to the village and passed them out to the kids. You should've seen that scene. WILD! I'm telling you.

"I noticed one little girl standing off to the side. She had to be about three, or four. Just a little bitty thing. Pretty as a button. She had the biggest and brightest eyes I think I've ever seen in such a tiny face. She was too timid, or too scared, to get into that mayhem, so I took one of the packages over to her. I knew it had a little doll in it. She tore into that thing, and you should have seen her face. There wasn't anything about her that wasn't smiling. I couldn't have asked much more out of Christmas than that.

"But here it is Christmas afternoon, and I'm lying on my bunk, stuffed to the gills with turkey and dressing—I even ate some fruitcake, just out of tradition, but it was yukky. Made me long for a slice of that fruitcake your mama makes with all those pecans and the little marshmallows in it. The cookies you made were terrific, though, and the pecan divinity was truly divine. I shared a little of it with some of my buddies but I'm hoarding the rest. I hope you liked your presents. I loved mine. But the only present I really want is you—and our baby. For that, I know I have to wait. But only 307 more days! I guess you'll just have to be my Halloween presents."

After signing with all his love, he added a P.S. "I've been thinking about names. If it's a girl, what would you think about naming her after Sandy?"

The January letters were filled with talk of Laurel's pregnancy, their coming child and his dreams for their lives together. At times he seemed to be hoping for a boy, at other times for a girl. Whichever it turned out to be, he was certain that their child would be brilliant and destined for a life of great accomplishment. "I may be getting a little ahead of myself," he joked, "but as much as I love Clemson, I'm thinking Harvard."

He also mentioned that he had made friends with the little girl to whom he had given the doll before Christmas. "She comes running every time she sees me, calling, 'Zheem! Zheem!' That's how she pronounces Jim. I didn't think she'd be able to handle Jimmy, so I just kept pointing at myself and saying, 'Jim,' and she picked right up on it. Still, she's doing better than I am. She pointed at herself and called out her name, but when I tried to pronounce it, she laughed and laughed. So I started calling her Smiley Eyes. I think she likes that better. I still haven't picked up much Vietnamese, but she sits in my lap and jabbers away, and I just smile and nod. I hope she's not asking me if I'm her daddy, or if I will put her through college. I try to take her a little something special every time I pass through the village. She is a doll. You would just love her to death. I'm going to send a picture of her soon."

Near the end of the month, Whitey wrote that he was beginning to feel a little guilty about the candy and gum he'd been passing out to the kids. "Some of them have such bad teeth," he wrote. "I bought a toothbrush and took it to Smiley Eyes, but I wasn't sure that she understood what she was supposed to do with it. She wanted gum—goom, she calls it. She loves Juicy Fruit. Of course, I gave her a whole pack. BIG, BIG smiles. She'd be perfect for a Juicy Fruit commercial."

The Tet Offensive began on January 31, catching American forces off guard and creating a whole new war. Heavy fighting was taking place throughout the country, and as casualties rapidly mounted, Americans were seeing the horrors of war on their TV screens as never before. The effect of the offensive was obvious in the last two letters Whitey wrote to his wife. A letter dated February 7 was uncharacteristically brief, but Whitey remained true to his optimism.

"I'm sorry I haven't been able to write. Things have been a little hectic here. I know that you have been hearing and seeing stuff in the news about what is happening, and I know how you worry, but you have no reason to. I am fine, just busier than usual. Things are not as bad here as they are in other parts of the country, so don't let your imagination get carried away, unless it's about how much I love you and our baby. That's one thing that even your fervid imagination can't make bigger than it is. And no matter how far away it may seem, the three of us will one day be together. That I promise."

The final letter was dated February 11. "Joy! Joy! Joy! After getting no mail at all for nearly two weeks, I suddenly have ten letters from you and that beautiful valentine. No, I haven't received the peanut butter fudge yet, but I can't wait for it to get here. I'm sure it will soon. I spent two hours just reading your letters over and over, and I could almost feel you here beside me. That is my fondest desire, to be beside you, to hold you and kiss you and tell you how very much I love you. Circumstances wouldn't allow me to get you a valentine, but I promise that will never happen again. Next year I will buy you valentines of satin, and roses galore and chocolates until you can eat no more. I may even write you a poem after a line like that. But until then this will just have to do."

Enclosed was a crudely drawn heart with an arrow through it. It had the look of a grammar school valentine. "To Laurel, my forever valentine," was scrawled across the top in a juvenile hand. It was signed, "With all my love, Howdy Doody."

Two more bundles from the shoe box held letters from men in Whitey's company. I only got through one, the first to arrive. After that, I didn't feel like going on. The letter was from a sergeant whose name I will withhold. It told the rest of the story.

Feb. 14, 1968

Dear Mrs. Black,

I'm not much at writing letters, and this is the hardest one I've ever tried to write. I was with Lt. Black when he was killed and I wanted you to know what happened.

We were passing through the village outside the base. I was driving and the lieutenant was in the seat next to me. We had never had trouble in the village before so it caught us by surprise when we began taking sniper fire. It all seemed to happen at once, real fast. I saw this little girl the lieutenant called Smiley Eyes. She dashed out from between two buildings just as I heard the first shots. Almost before I could hit the brake, the lieutenant had jumped out of the vehicle and was running toward her. He snatched her up and was trying to get to cover when he was hit. He took three rounds. Nobody could get to him until we had cleared out the snipers. It wasn't but a few minutes, but when we got to him he was already gone. The little girl was under him, and we heard her moaning and

"The lieutenant ... snatched her up and was
trying to get to cover ... "

thought she might have been hit too but she hadn't. I thought she might have known about the snipers and was trying to warn us. But she had a little pink toothbrush in her hand, and some of the people in the village told us that she wanted to show Lt. Black that she had learned to brush her teeth. He had given her the toothbrush. There is no doubt that your husband saved that little girl's life, and there is not a man in this company that does not hold him to be a hero. He was a good man and a brave man, and a lot of us have shed many a tear over his loss. I know that none of us will ever forget him. All of us want you to know that our thoughts and our prayers are with you. I am enclosing a photo that I made of Lt. Black and the little girl a few weeks ago. I had promised to give him one, and I know he would want you to have it. I think it is the last picture that was made of him.

The photo was missing from the envelope.

Eleven

"So what did you think?" Sandy asked, when I handed back the box of letters the next morning.

"I think you must be awfully proud of him."

"I am."

"I can't say I was surprised by what he did," I said. "I would have expected him to react that way. I'm sure he didn't have a moment's hesitation, no thought of danger to himself. He was just thinking of saving that little girl."

"And maybe of me," she said. "And Sandy."

"I thought of that, too," I said. "I'm sure

you're right."

"I've got something else I wanted to show you," she said.

She fetched a small frame from a nearby table and handed it to me. Inside, covered by glass, pinned to blue satin, were three military medals: the Purple Heart, Bronze Star and Silver Star. Only the Congressional Medal of Honor is a higher award for valor than the Silver Star.

"They had a ceremony at Fort Benning and presented these to my mother," she said. "She had them framed and put them on the wall in her bedroom beneath a portrait of my dad so that was the first thing she saw when she woke up every morning.

"He got the Bronze Star for something that happened before he saved the little girl. The Silver Star and the Purple Heart were for that."

I had read about the earlier incident at breakfast when I went through the remaining letters that the men in Whitey's company had written to his wife after his death. The letters made clear just how much Whitey had been keeping to himself about the war. He had seen lots of combat, especially in the last two weeks of his life.

In one firefight, a new man in the company, an eighteen-year-old private, froze in panic when a man near him went down. He was exposed, unable to move, shaking all over, his eyes locked in terror on his fallen comrade. Whitey had put himself at risk to get the man to cover, and after going to help the wounded man, had returned to calm and reassure the panicked private.

"He was the kind of person who could just look at you, or touch you on the shoulder and make you feel that everything was going to be all right," one man in his unit had written. "After I was wounded, he stayed with me until the med-evac chopper came. He was joking and even had me laughing despite how scared I was and all the pain I was in. 'You've got a million-dollar wound,' he told me. 'You'll fly home on this one. You sure you don't want to trade places?' I was in the hospital when I heard he had been killed, and my first thought was that I would have traded places with him if I could. It should have been me, not him. Sometimes it seems like it's always the best ones who are taken."

All the letters spoke of the men's grief over Whitey's death and of the respect, admiration and affection they held for him. Almost every one had a personal story of some kindness Whitey had shown, or something funny, or meaningful, he'd said or done.

"He wouldn't ask you to do anything that he wouldn't do himself," one noted. "He was a real leader. He knew what was important and what wasn't. He wouldn't give anybody a hard time unless they were slacking off or doing something that would endanger others."

"He wasn't like other officers," another wrote. "He was somebody you could talk to when you couldn't talk to anybody else. He always made you feel better."

Sandy and I were still talking about the letters as we drove toward Easley a little later,

Sandy at the wheel of her mini-van, Laurel in the back seat with the Cookie Monster.

"I still take them out and read them at least once a year," Sandy said, usually in February, about the time of my dad's death. They always make me feel good about him."

"What do you think about the Vietnam War now?" I asked.

"I try not to think about it. I know all the pain my mother went through because of that war; she never got over it. And it wasn't exactly easy for me not having a daddy and seeing my mother grieve for the rest of her life. When you've been through something like that, you don't want to think that it was all for nothing."

"He did save that little girl," I pointed out.

"But if we hadn't been there, she wouldn't have needed him to save her, would she?"

I couldn't answer that.

"Like I say," she said. "I try not to think about it."

"Have you been to the Vietnam Memorial?" I asked.

She nodded. "It was one of the most emotional experiences of my life. You know, the week my daddy died was the bloodiest of the war. Five hundred and forty-three Americans were killed in Vietnam that week. But my daddy was the only one whose name I ever knew. Then I got up there to that memorial and there were all those names, thousands and thousands of names, every one somebody's son, or brother, or daddy, or daughter, or sister, and every one a story just as sad as my daddy's. And that was just the people on our side. There were many, many thousands more who died in that war whose names we'll never know. So many sad stories. It made me realize that I wasn't the only child who grew up without a daddy because of that war. It helped to put things in perspective."

We rode in silence for a few moments.

"He gave his life that another might live."

"Have you been there?" she asked.

"No, but now I know I have to go."

"I think you'll find it deeply moving," she said.

"I never dreamed that if I ever found out what happened to Whitey it would be like this," I told her. "I wanted him to be well and prosperous with a happy family, maybe a grandchild or two. I guess I also wanted him to be the one giving the angel dolls to the hospital. And not just for the sake of my book," I added quickly.

"Well, he does have a happy family," Sandy said, her mood brightening.

"And an awfully cute granddaughter," I added, turning to smile at Laurel in the back seat.

"And you're not too far wrong about the angel dolls either," Sandy said.

"What do you mean?" I asked, caught again by surprise.

"He did do it once," she said. "My mother was a pediatric nurse, you know, and she told me that whenever my dad came by the hospital in Columbus, she would find him going from room to room, joking and laughing with the sick children.

"Just before the last Christmas they spent together, my mother was looking for something, I don't remember what, but she opened the trunk of the car. There were these dolls that had been made to look like angels, six of them. She had no idea what they were for; she thought they must be for some kind of surprise my dad was planning, and she didn't say anything to him about it. She didn't want to spoil it for him.

"Because she was still new on the staff, she had to work Christmas Eve, and when she got to the children's ward that afternoon, there were those dolls in a big cardboard box with an unsigned, typed note that said, 'Please give these to any child who needs a guardian angel for Christmas.'

"My mother told me that when she got

home that night, she said to my dad, 'The most wonderful thing happened at the hospital today.' Then she went on to tell him about the dolls and how she and other staff members had taken them around to the sickest children, and how happy they and their families had been. 'I thought it was the sweetest thing for somebody to do,' she told him. And all he said was that he wished he could have been there to see the children. Never said a word about having anything to do with it. And my mother never let on that she knew.

"Mother knew that Dad had been hurt deeply by Sandy's death, but like I told you last night, she didn't know about the doll, so she never really understood why he had done that. And she didn't understand why he wanted to keep it secret. But now I do, because of your book. So you see why it was such a gift to me?"

"I'm glad," I said, "but that still doesn't explain the angel dolls I wrote about."

She smiled. "That's because you haven't let me finish my story."

"Oops," I said sheepishly. "Sorry."

"After the men who served with my dad in Vietnam got back home, one by one they came to visit my mother. "I think almost every one who wrote to her eventually came, those who survived, I mean. They told her lots of stories about him.

"One of the stories my mother told them was about the angel dolls he'd left at the hospital."

"So that was how it started," I said.

"Mmm-uh. Somehow, some of them got together later and decided they wanted to do something to honor my dad, and they called and asked my mom what she thought about them donating angel dolls to a children's hospital every Christmas.

"She thought it was a wonderful idea— so long as they never let anybody know where they were coming from, or why. That was the only way it could truly honor my dad, she thought. They started doing it in 1970, and they've been doing it ever since.

"It doesn't cost all that much. Just a few thousand dollars a year. One of those guys started an electronics company after he got out of the Army and he's got more money than all of us could ever spend. He's the main organizer, and he could do it all by himself, but the other guys still want to be part of it. They send their money every year. Most of them kept up with my mother all through the years, too. Some of them used to bring their families to visit us. They would come near Christmas and bring presents. They sent me Christmas presents right up until I got out of high school. Some of them still call every Christmas."

"What a great story," I said, "but, boy, have you put me in a dilemma."

"Not as much as you think," she said with a smile. "I wasn't even going to tell you about this. I knew you'd want to write about it. But last night at dinner when you began telling us how people were responding to your book, and especially how some of them were making angel dolls and taking them to hospitals, I had second thoughts.

"I prayed about it when I went to bed, and I know this sounds weird, but I still talk to my daddy, even though I never knew him. And what's even weirder—and I've never told this to anybody, not even Gene—is that he talks back to me. So we had a little talk last night. And that was when I decided that I was going to tell you.

"In a way, you had already revealed my dad's secret without knowing it. And I knew that if you did write more about it and it caused even a few more people to love a little more, or to give a little more, especially to children, my dad would be all for it.

"Still, I was concerned about what his friends from Vietnam might think. So before you came this morning I made a call. As long as you don't reveal their names, or the hospital, it's okay with them."

"They don't have a thing to worry about," I said.

We had reached the entrance to Greenlawn Cemetery and Sandy slowed to make the turn. Pines dotted the hillside, but mostly the cemetery was open to the sunny autumn sky. Near the crest, Sandy pulled the mini-van onto the grass. As she fetched fresh flowers from the back of the van, I unhooked Laurel's seat belt and lifted her out.

"Let me help you with those," I said, and Sandy handed me two of the pots of flowers she had arranged. Laurel wanted her Cookie Monster before we walked the short distance to the markers at the top of the hill. Four graves were in the plot where we were headed. Three had conventional granite markers, but over one presided a marble angel three and a half feet high, standing atop a pedestal, the white marble darkened by age and grit. As we drew nearer, I saw that Whitey lay between his wife and his sister, his mother on Sandy's other side.

"We come and clean the stones every Easter," Sandy said, stooping to put flowers on her mother's grave, "but it doesn't take long before they're all dirty again."

I stopped before the angel. "An angel

on earth, now an angel in heaven," read the inscription.

"My mother said she only had a tiny marker at first," Sandy said, coming to stand beside me, but my dad bought that angel when he was in high school and paid for it in monthly payments with the money he earned at his jobs."

I left one of my pots of flowers at the foot of the angel, and as Sandy placed her remaining flowers on the grave of Whitey's mother, I stepped over to his stone.

James Saunders Black
1st Lt., U.S. Army
Killed in Action
Nov. 11, 1941 - Feb. 13, 1968
He gave his life that another might live

Just above the inscription, inset into the granite, encased in heavy waterproofed glass was a fading black-and-white photograph. In it, Whitey was in full field uniform, bareheaded, seated on his helmet, and at his knee was a pretty little bright-eyed Vietnamese girl, both smiling broadly. I stooped to place the flowers where both could see them.

"I never even knew his middle name," I said, as Sandy stepped up to put an arm around me. We stood for a while in silence. I lingered as Sandy and Laurel started back to the mini-van.

"Why was that man crying?" I heard Laurel ask.

"Because he loved your grandpa," her mother told her.

"Love doesn't make you cry," Laurel said.

"Sometimes it does."

"You see the smoke stack over there?" Sandy asked when I walked down to the mini-van. "That was Easley Mill, where my dad's mother, and his grandmother and grandfather all worked. It's been closed for six or seven years now. And those lights over there by the water tower, that was the ballpark where my dad played on the mill team. This building right down here at the foot of the hill," she went on, pointing to a small aging structure now used for storage, "that was The Drive-In where my dad worked when he was in high school.

"One Easter before my mother died, we were up here cleaning the stones, and a man came wandering over and introduced himself. He had worked with my dad at The Drive-In. He had people up here, too. He told us that sometimes when my dad got off work late at night, he would come up here and just sit, all alone, beside Sandy's grave for an hour or two."

"I'm sure he was never alone," I said.

After we got back to Sandy's house, I offered an invitation. "I want you to come and visit," I said. "I'll take you to Thomasville and show you all the places from the book."

"We'd love to," she said.

"Can I go, too, Mommy?" Laurel asked.

"They'd better bring you," I told her, then turned back to her mother. "Can you come before Christmas?"

"Just tell us when," she said. "We'll be there."

A half hour later, I was nearly twenty miles down Interstate 385 toward Columbia when I found myself taking an exit, crossing over the highway, and returning the way I had come. I drove straight back to Greenlawn Cemetery and left a copy of *The Angel Doll* at the foot of Whitey's stone.

Part 4

Christmas

Heap on more wood!—the wind is chill;
But let it whistle as it will,
We'll keep our Christmas merry still.

Sir Walter Scott

$\mathcal{T}welve$

"So that's the famous Big Chair," Sandy said.

"That's it."

The biggest Duncan Phyfe chair in the world, eighteen feet tall, made of concrete, stood atop a twelve-foot limestone base by the mainline railroad tracks at the center of my hometown of Thomasville, a big magnolia serving as its backdrop. It was erected as the symbol of the town's pre-eminence in furniture. The Chair City, Thomasville proudly called itself.

"They dedicated it in 1951, the year Sandy died and your dad and his mom moved away," I said. "Miss America had her picture made in it before the Christmas parade that year. The fire department put up a ladder for her, and all the firemen modestly turned their heads as she climbed up to the seat, because she had one hand on the ladder and the other holding her skirt as tight as she could get it. But Whitey and I got as close as we could and watched the whole thing. It was an exhilarating experience for ten-year-old boys."

Gene chuckled.

"Quite a few Miss Americas climbed up into that chair over the years," I continued. "We always had Miss America in our Christmas parade. But it was Lyndon Johnson who really made it famous."

The President was on a whistle-stop tour along the Southern Railroad during the election of 1964, I explained. When the train stopped briefly in Thomasville, Johnson could not resist the Big Chair. He climbed onto it and waved his Stetson as photographers clicked away. The photo not only appeared in newspapers everywhere but in *Life* magazine.

"Even that chair wasn't big enough to hold *his* ego," I said.

"I've often wondered if my dad might not still be alive if he'd never been President," Sandy observed, a slight edge to her voice.

We were in my Pathfinder, Gene and I in the front seat, Linda, Sandy and Laurel in the back, beginning our tour of Thomasville. It was the Saturday before Christmas. The Medlins had first driven to our house near Asheboro, arriving in early afternoon. We had loaded into the Pathfinder for the thirty-minute drive to Thomasville.

All tours of Thomasville begin at the Big Chair. Some begin and end here, for there is little else to attract visitors except for Thomasville Furniture's factory outlet store, just across the railroad tracks and a few blocks to the east. But memories guided this tour, and it would include many stops.

Saturday was the primary shopping day in Thomasville when Whitey and I were kids. Both the factory workers and the country people crowded downtown then, and the final Saturday before Christmas enticed throngs to Main and Salem Streets.

But now Thomasville's center of commerce was clustered in strip shopping centers around Interstate 85. Downtown Thomasville had seen some dismal years before an effort had been made to revive it. Some buildings had been torn down. New parking lots and miniature parks had been created. The railroad tracks had been lined with shrubbery and trees. Flower beds had been installed. And gradually downtown came back.

Now, if not exactly thriving, it was at least vital again. Only a few buildings remained vacant. Hudson-Belk, our biggest department store, was now an antique mall. But I still saw downtown as it had been when I was ten. The herb shop on the corner was still Mann's Drugs. The florist shop was still Peace's Cafe. City Hall with its impressive granite columns remained First National Bank.

As we drove slowly northward on Salem Street, I pointed out where the Rexall Drug Store had been, where we went to read comic books and buy freshly made orangeades and Cherry Smashes. The Palace Theater was just down the street, across from Murphy's Grocery, where I'd held my first real job after my paper routes. Although the buildings remained, nobody seeing them now would ever guess that they had housed a theater and a grocery.

"Boys who ran away from the orphanage had a hideout on top of Belk's," I said, "and they knew how to sneak into the Palace through a basement window. They tried to get Whitey and me to do it, but we were too scared."

A right turn on East Guilford brought us to a brick building that was now a printing company. "This was the Tribune," I said, turning into the narrow alley beside it. "This was where Whitey and I had our fight. We came here straight from school every Tuesday and Thursday. Those were the days the paper came out."

I stopped at the back of the building. Double metal doors, painted blue, offered entry at ground level, next to a small loading dock built of cinder blocks. Nothing here looked much different than I remembered it from those days. "The old flat-bed press sat just inside those doors," I said. "It was always breaking down. Sometimes it would be after dark before we got our papers and could start delivering them."

"Oh, no," Linda said, "he's going to start on the hardships of his paper route. The snow drifts would be six-feet deep and he had to use old socks for gloves, and he only had one ear muff that he had to keep switching from ear to ear...."

"Stop, stop," I said, laughing. "I'll spare you, I promise. See those stairs leading down to the back of that building over there? That was the Pioneer Restaurant, the fanciest restaurant in Thomasville. That was our shortcut to Rexall Drugs. We'd cut through the storage room and the kitchen, around the counter and through the dining room. All these kids just passing through, and I never remember anybody saying a word about it."

An adjoining alley led us back to Main Street. I turned to the right and took the first open parking spot. It happened to be in front of the building that once had been McLellan's Five & Dime. The building now stood empty, a "For Rent" sign in the center window. "That window right there was where the doll was on display when your dad first saw it," I told Sandy, pointing to the one on the right.

We all got out and peered into the empty store. Only I was seeing it as it once had been. Only I could see Whitey's happy face as he emerged from the store carrying the doll.

"There's one place we have to go into," I said. "It's just down the street."

Tasty Bakery was in a brick building with an imitation stone front, one of only three downtown businesses that had remained unchanged all these years (the others were City Shoe Shop and the Boston Store, a fashionable clothing shop just across the railroad tracks). The bakery had two big windows where fake wedding and birthday cakes were displayed, and I recalled how the owners once exhibited special cakes heralding all of

Thomasville's major events. People actually went downtown just to see those cakes.

"Whitey and I saved our nickels for this place," I said as we all herded inside. "I usually got the brownie with walnuts, or the cream horn. Whitey loved those chocolate cream doughnuts. I bet he could've eaten a half dozen at one time, but we usually only had enough money for one. Whitey always saved half of his to take home to Sandy—well, almost always."

I introduced myself and all the others to the friendly woman who now ran the place, and she got up a selection of goodies for us, including some colorful Christmas cookies for Sandy.

"And I need a chess pie," I said, and turned to explain to Gene and Sandy. "This place makes the best chess pies in all the world. We'll have it for dinner."

We departed with Christmas wishes and soon were crossing the railroad tracks again at the Big Chair.

Tennis courts occupied the site where Main Street School had been. The school had been torn down years ago. Only the old gym remained, now the town's recreation center. I had been in the fifth grade at that school, Whitey in the fourth, when he had moved away.

"I'll show you a picture of it when we get home," I told Sandy. "I can still see every inch of that building in my mind. It was for grades one through twelve when your dad was living here. But they built a new school the next year and I went to it for two years, then came back here."

Memories came swarming back as they always did when I turned onto Fifth Avenue. I recalled the people who had lived in the houses long ago. "Jack Gilliam had one of the first TVs in Thomasville," I said, pointing to a house on the left. "We kids would hide in the shrubbery around his porch on summer nights and watch through the screen door."

I stopped the car. "This was Billy Barnes'

house," I said.

"His mother made the doll," Sandy remembered.

"She still lives in Thomasville," I said. "But not here. Billy's dad built a clubhouse for us in the back yard. It was right back there where that little shed is now. We had our Cub Scout meetings there. Billy had an eight-millimeter movie projector and we would show Castle films, little black & white silent movies with Red Ryder, Hopalong Cassidy, Bud Abbott and Lou Costello."

I could hardly recognize the little house where I had grown up, between the Joneses and the Becks, so drastically had it changed. Somebody had added a second story to it.

"When I used to come by here fifteen or twenty years ago, before it was remodeled, it always seemed so much smaller than it did when I lived here," I said.

An asphalt parking lot for the recreation center now filled the entire vacant lot on Taylor Street that we kids had turned into a baseball field.

"The big kids, teenagers, all had the school ballfield inside the fence across the road there," I said. "They wouldn't let us play. So we just turned this lot into a ballfield of our own. We put down bases and built a backstop out of old chicken wire. We even had bleachers we made from cement blocks and old boards. We didn't have any idea who owned the land. We just appropriated it, but nobody ever tried to stop us from playing here.

"Whitey was an all-around better player than I was. He was a ground-ball hitter, and he could really run and field. He was a little fanatic about his glove. He wouldn't let anybody else use it. Not many people could, I guess, since he was left-handed. But he took great care of it, always kept the pocket oiled, had a special place for it in his room. It was his proudest possession.

"I don't mean to brag, but I was a home-run hitter. A regular Babe Ruth. Me and Chester Myers. We had a contest going to see who could hit the most home runs. I think he finally won. He was stockier and stronger than I was. But I could hit for a skinny kid."

Noah Ledford's store, one of mine and Whitey's favorite spots, was our next stop, but only weeds and scrubby bushes grew where it once stood. I could only describe it, but that was no problem for it, too, remained vivid in my mind, even down to the arrangement of the candy in the big glass-enclosed counter. And who could forget Noah, ancient and bent, with a huge beak of a nose, a crotchedy old man, dipping snuff and snarling impatiently at all us kids?

Only a short distance away, I turned onto Carolina Avenue and we soon arrived at the site of the decrepit little rental house where Whitey had lived with his mother and Sandy. Now a factory stood there. The nearby lumber yard remained, but it was enclosed in a heavy fence, the lumber sheltered in incredibly high stacks under row after row of huge sheds supported by steel beams, no longer a place where boys could play.

I pulled over by the feeder railroad line

and was describing things as they had been nearly half a century earlier.

"Where was my dad on Christmas morning when he told you what happened to Sandy?" Sandy asked.

"Right down there, maybe about fifty yards," I said, pointing down the railroad tracks to the east.

"Would it be all right if I got out?" she asked.

"Sure."

"Want me to come with you, Hon?" Gene said.

"No, I'll just be a minute."

"Can I come, Mommy?" Laurel asked.

"No, you stay here," her dad said. "She won't be long."

Sandy walked along the tracks to the spot where I had pointed, then stood for a while, her back to us, before returning.

"That was the hardest part of the book for me," she said, after she was back in her seat. "Being here made it even more real."

We rode mostly in silence on the drive back to Asheboro, Sandy lost in thought.

Thirteen

We had an early dinner. Gene and Sandy were facing a three-and-a-half-hour drive back home and didn't want to be on the road late. Both had duties at church the next morning. After finishing the chess pie to much acclaim, we gathered by the Christmas tree in the living room.

"Are we going to open presents now?" Laurel asked.

"Honey, that's not polite," Sandy admonished.

"But that's exactly what we're going to do," I said.

Laurel clapped her hands in excitement, then glanced warily at her mother.

Linda had bought small gifts for Sandy and Gene. She let Laurel give them to her parents, while I fetched the biggest present from beneath the tree. Linda had wrapped it in gold paper and festooned it with gold ribbons.

"Let's see whose name is on this one," I said. "I think it says Laurel."

"It's big," she said, as I placed it on the floor beside her. "Can I open it now, Mommy?"

"Sure," she said, smiling.

Laurel tore into the wrapping, then removed the lid from the white box.

"Here, let me help," said her mother, joining her on the floor.

Together, they lifted the tissue to reveal the doll.

"Ooooh...." Laurel said, clearly enchanted.

"Isn't it beautiful?" Sandy asked, lifting it from the box. She stood it before Laurel,

"Oh, Mommy, is it really mine?"

straightening the gown, adjusting the fragile, glittery wings and the drooping gold halo.

"Oh, Mommy, is it really mine?"

"It's really yours," I said. "I think it was always meant to be."

"It's a very special doll," her mother said. "You'll have to take very good care of it."

"I will, Mommy. I won't let anybody play with it and I won't spill grape juice on it."

"She ruined one of her Barbie outfits," Sandy explained, rolling her eyes.

"Can't you say thank you?" she said to Laurel.

Laurel glanced from her mother to me, grinning mischievously. "You're welcome," she said, and as I laughed she ran to my arms and gave me a hug.

"Don't we have something for the Bledsoes?" Sandy said, sending Laurel running to a shopping bag her father had brought in earlier.

"Here, wait a minute, better let me help you," Gene said, hurrying after her. "I'm afraid you might break one of those." He removed the smaller package, which he handed to Linda, then gave a larger one to Laurel. "Here, you can take this one to Jerry."

Linda opened hers to find a crystal hummingbird. I recognized mine as soon as I tore into the box. It was a boy's baseball glove, an old one, a lefty's. "Jimmy B." had been inked on the strap. I was taken aback seeing it again.

"I'm honored," I said, "but I can't keep this. It's too important to you."

"He would want you to have it," Sandy said. "I know I do."

"Thank you," I said, turning the glove in my hand.

"Somebody's been keeping the pocket oiled," I noted, glancing at Gene.

"Just takes a dab or two every now and

then," he replied.

I tried pulling the glove on my right hand but it wouldn't fit.

"It's too little," Laurel said. "You can't catch with it."

"It'll be just fine," I assured her, popping the pocket with my fist. "It's just for catching memories now."

A short time later, we were all in the driveway as our guests prepared to leave.

"Can the angel doll ride beside me?" Laurel asked, as her father strapped her into her seat.

"Maybe if we take off her wings," he said.

"She'll have to wear her seat belt," Laurel announced.

"I don't think angels need seat belts."

"It's the law, Daddy," Laurel responded with a tone of exasperation.

"Okay," he sighed, and with a shrug he fetched the doll and carefully hooked her in.

We exchanged hugs and goodbyes.

"Promise you'll come back next Christmas?"

"I promise," Sandy replied. "We'll bring the doll and make it a tradition."

I knew that she meant it, but all too well I knew how time and good intentions slip away when you're young, how easy it is to lose touch with friends, whether new or treasured.

"I hope so," I said.

Fourteen

Christmas Eve fell on Wednesday and in late afternoon Erik arrived from his teaching job in Tennessee. Home for Christmas. Our little family triangle reconnected for the holiday. Shortly after dark we drove to Greensboro to greet friends, exchange gifts, eat and make merry at the home of Stan and Kay Swofford. I'm "Uncle" Jerry to the Swofford children, Katy and Andrew, and that grants me the privilege of reading one of their Christmas stories each year before they're off to bed.

Back home by eleven, we began our own little Christmas Eve ritual.

First, I read from the edition of *A Christmas Carol* illustrated by Grandma Moses, the corners well chewed by Erik's first puppy,

Scotty, more than a quarter of a century earlier. This year I also added *The Littlest Angel*. Linda was dozing as I turned to Truman Capote's *A Christmas Memory*.

I made it almost to the end before my voice broke, as usual, leaving me unable to go on, and Erik reached for the book and finished the story as I dabbed at my eyes with a handkerchief. All part of the ritual.

Erik put down the book and kissed his mother on the forehead, causing her to stir.

"Merry Christmas," he said.

"Merry Christmas," she responded, as if she had been alert all the while.

He hugged us both and went off to bed.

Linda and I stood looking at the tree she had decorated so beautifully, each with an arm around the other, the colorful lights flickering and dancing in rhythm. From the stereo, Johnny Mathis sang softly..."What child is thi-is...."

Our presents for each other and for

Erik were still piled beneath the tree in paper shiny and ribbon bright. We would not open them until morning.

"Seems to be an empty spot without the doll," I observed. She had stood by our tree each Christmas for twenty-two years and her absence was conspicuous.

"But surely not in your heart," Linda said, looking up at me with a little smile.

"No, that's brimming full."

She kissed me. "Merry Christmas."

"Merry Christmas to you."

We did not need to speak our love, but we did.

"Coming to bed?" she asked, although she knew I always stayed up well past midnight on Christmas Eve, for Santa yet had presents to retrieve from secret places.

"In a little while," I replied.

A short time later, chores accomplished, I sat in the recliner by my reading light, Mutt's book, *Christmas in My Bones*, in hand, and flipped to one of my favorite passages:

Why is a candle brighter at Christmas time? Why is a fire on the hearth warmer, a friend dearer, a family nearer? Why is a book given at Christmas a cheerier companion than the same or another volume in another month? What is the color of the sky at night and what can gauge the radiance of Christmas stars?

I am sure that these things are true and good. I cannot answer the questions.

I expect there are no answers and no need for them. For Christmas is a mystery, the brightest, merriest mystery of all time. And mysteries are not made of answers.

Love, too, is one of those mysteries not made of answers, and Christmas *is* love, the proof that it exists, the promise that it will endure, passed from heart to heart, transcending time and space. Whitey and Mutt knew that, each in his own way, and had made it a gift to me, a gift to be celebrated with all the joy it was meant to bring.

"Merry Christmas, old friends," I said aloud. "I hope you're as proud of me as I am of both of you. I miss you and love you dearly."

For just a moment I thought I heard something—Mutt's warm and distinctive chuckle. Perhaps it was the wind. Or just a Christmas wish.